CELLPHONE TEXTING CAN BE FUN

Sex class teachers should read this book, then have there
students read it, because the numbers are so high.
All around the world!

CHUCK SIMON

To order additional copies of this book, contact:
Xlibris
1-888-795-4274
www.Xlibris.com
Orders@Xlibris.com

ISBN: 978-1-9845-8127-3 (sc)
ISBN: 978-1-9845-8126-6 (e)

Print information available on the last page

Rev. date: 05/27/2020

CELL PHONE TEXTING CAN BE FUN

Based on a true - tear jerker story

First edition / Science Fiction

by Chuck Simon

Everyone can do this

Sex class teachers should read this book, then have their students read it, because the numbers are so high. All around the world!

Everyone Can Do This?

As a 64-year-old man, I discovered ways to analyze people. When analyzing the eye contact and body language of men and women under the age of 30, certain patterns arise. This book is about patterns in body language and eye contact of individuals under the age of 30 and how they interact with adults. Straight children look at Straight people and want to learn from them. All children that are straight look at Straight people like me: we all are born to be Straight, lesbian or gay.
If you know someone who is gay and do not know how to tell him just have him read my book.

Why does this happen? Orbs are commutating with each other in ways we currently don't understand. When we die there is a real possibility that we then become an Orb. Some Christians believe Orbs are real, however, the bible never mentions Orbs.

What we don't understand is why adults over 30 years old don't look at Straight people as freely as those under 30 do.

Now that there over 7.6 billon people on planet earth, times are changing Lesbians are starting to color their hair with rainbow colors to attract other Lesbians and starting to wear dresses rather than slacks.

Lesbians and gays are using Face book to advertise their sexual preference. They are using symbols in their photos like peace signs with their fingers, pretending to kiss those of the same sex without touching lips, and using both their hands to make a heart. These are some of the new ways they are advertising their sexual preferences.

There is a big drawback– if they use Face book for these types of exploits it is possible their siblings or their parents could see it. As a way to get around that, many use a different name on Face book.

There are **3** kinds of people on planet earth.

For gay men it is obvious they want to have a relationship with another man, get married, and adopt children.

For lesbian Girls it is obvious they want to have a relationship with another Girl, get married, and adopt children.

Straight people get married and have children— like me.

When children look at Straight people (it is in their eyes) their heads turn and their eyes directly focus into our eyes as though they want to stare at Straight people for a moment. If their parents tell their children to pay attention, children pay attention to what they are told too. If their parents want them to look at something new, they look, but children are curious (why) and if they get a chance they'll try to stare at us Straight people.

Only Straight children look at Straight people while they're inside buildings or outside, and this happens only if they are not gay or Lesbian. It is very fascinating; children sense me and automatically turn their heads to look at me while they keep walking with their mom and dad. They try to keep looking at me. I believe they want to watch me and learn from us Straight people.

This is much harder to see in Humans over the age of 30. However, I will still be able to identify them. All the new people I teach this to need to practice. It took me around 64 years to understand this gift and I am still learning, your feedback will be helpful. A good place to practice this is at the Mall of America, other shopping centers, parks that have playgrounds, or other places where lots of people go.

Children and those 30 years old or younger will look at me, but only if they are Straight. In another words, young people have are curious and want to spend time understanding many new things in life. They can feel something in the air.

Straight people get married and have children. However, gay men and Girls find themselves embarrassed with the situation they are in. Many Girls know they are Lesbians and men know they are gay even if they are married to a member of the opposite sex. Their parents expect them to get married and have children.

My studies have shown me Girls or women (Lesbians) want to have relationships with men to be satisfied.

ORBS

It is my hope to share my findings and observations with scientific communities and the general public to improve our understanding of the natural universe.

There is an ongoing debate, or at least spirited discussion, among ghost hunters and paranormal investigators about the validity of Orbs as paranormal evidence. Orbs are anomalous spots that sometimes show up in photographs. Most are white, some are multicolored, some look solid, and others appear textured.

"Orbs" have been dismissed as paranormal. However, in the near future their existence will become more apparent.

Antony van Leeuwenhoek did not initially consider himself a scientist and neither did I before my work with Orbs in photography; our discoveries were purely by accident.

Science is advancing all the time, but only rarely is the opportunity afforded to discover a science that is entirely separate from other works.

I am overwhelmed with this project, especially with all the different kinds of Orbs. The hardest thing for me is I am doing this project on my own. I would prefer to work with others as a team effort.

Orbs are here because of digital technology. We can see them at night or in the dark and even when there is daylight outside they are all around us all the time. I believe Orbs are communicating with other Orbs. This is why Straight children look at us. Somehow the Orbs are communicating in unbelievable ways through us. Or could it be because of the Paranormal?

My observations are showing me Orbs cannot control us through closed car windows, shopping, store widows, or house windows!

God gave most of us five senses. Sight, hearing, smell, taste, and touch. That is what we have as individuals. After we are born we are taught by our parents, then school, then college and institutions. After that we have to look at our world as individuals based on our education and our five senses.

I think when we die we will become Orbs. All living things could become Orbs someday. There is a way we can prove this. To do so, you have to use a digital camera to take a picture every second or faster at animals while they are being slaughtered. For example, we eat chickens. In a place where chickens are slaughtered use a digital camera to take a picture every second or faster than splice them together to make a movie and see if Orbs come out of their bodies. Then try pigs, cows, fish, and then possibly Humans.

Google Orbs then look through the results. This will help you understand there are many different types of Orbs.

What I am talking about can only be seen with digital photography.

I was at a restaurant with my wife's friends. All her friends are Straight; I can tell by the way they all interact together. There was a young Girl there, around 4 years old, and she is Straight too. This was so amazing, we all watch each other knowing we are all the same but I did not tell them about this new way of understanding sexual orientation. It is in our eyes, our heads do turn but it is our eyes that look directly and focus into each other's eyes. I asked one older Girl if she understood Synchronicity and she said we could see on some kind of parallel with each other.

Anyone goes in the nut house we are automatically bipolar. Rock stars are bipolar too so am I poor us.

All women should be called Girls!

I spent 3 mounts over the last 2 years in a mental hospital that I will call the nut house of no criminal offences because of freedom of speech. They can hold us for as long as 21 days no more than that; they will be put under contract for six mounts and given drugs that will decrease the ability for sex like me Unhappy me! Girls can just show a cop there cell phone and they will put that man in the not house. In the mental hospital the Girl nurses said "it is inappropriate to pretty talk to them. So I said "it is inappropriate to tell a Girl she is fat or ugly" I got no response from them in another words I kept pretty talking to them and they had no complaints. The entire Girl staff did this, I think the male person that or professor in collage is wrong. He should teach them fat and ugly is inappropriate.

30% of the people in the nut house are prostitutes or hookers. 30% are on mood altering drugs and 30% need some guidance to get them out.

This subject should be tough in schools for ages 13 to 14 or older in sex class. I think Lesbians and gays will be told at this age because statistics will show (some day) in older Lesbians knowing they are Lesbians will not want to conceive a child. So young lesbian children will ask mom and dad to get tubes tied and gays will get clipped. The governments from around the world should pay for this procedure if there parents agree! Straight are the only ones that will want children except adoption for Lesbians and gays but, Lesbians could have a baby accidently and so could gays.

33.33% lesbian, 33.33% Straight, 33.33% gay, on planet earth we happened to be born this way.

Hookers can get there birth control drugs, sleeping aids in the hospital but these aids cause them to sleep way to much with not exercise they will become fat within five years. Stay with their case worker and psychiatrist through their entire life or at end of the contract no more drugs.

The first thing people will do is if they are a lesbian or gay is look into a mirror and look at their pupil in their eyes because it will be the first time in their life, their eyes will see their own pupils one is bigger than the other. You see Lesbians and gays will not look directly into the center of a camera lens until they admit in there harts they are Lesbians or gay and they will not look directly into a Straight persons eyes for some reason.

Gay men and Lesbians are lazy but after they read my book they will be more productive in the modern world.

It is important to understand Lesbians and gays, most of time, look to the right and or left when possible.

If you ask a lesbian if she is a lesbian? Her eyes will not change.

If you say or tell her "you are a lesbian" her eyes will go Straight.

Same with gays, but if a Straight man or gay man calls a gay "you are a gay" his eyes will change; If someone calls me gay I think first then look directly into their eyes and say "no way are you wrong "Ask a lesbian Girl to look into a big mirror with you. Ask her to look at the center of her eyes she will roll her eyes and she will say "I do not want to." then say you are a lesbian she will stare at you then have her look at the center of her eyes then she will. Practice on other Girls to help prove this is real.

After Lesbians or gays read this your eyes will change. All new Lesbians or gay people that read their eyes will change to Straight after you read this book.

If you are a lesbian or gay and have read this book your eyes will go Straight like Straight people like me for the rest of their lives.

Alan my son told me yesterday as soon as gay and Lesbian are 13 years old they know and understand he is proud to say I am gay the same thing happens to Lesbians. For me it is hard for me to understand? Lesbians and gays just simply understand it; Straight like me will never change.

Do you Girls know anyone that is texting you the wrong way like the pore Girls at Twin City Federal Bank (TCF) bank and Valley Fair, they are controlled by men. I have no trespassing orders from them now. Pore Girls, I learned how to help them as of now.

If Girls are unhappy with sex texting then simply show there cell phone to the police and the police will put him in the mental hospital for 3 weeks then you Girls will be happy!! This is a law.

What we need to do to the TCF bank is simple. Now Goldie is very unhappy with the men supervisors' at the bank but as soon as she reads this she will know how to handle the men at the bank. After people read this book their eyes in their head will change. This book is telling everyone this latest book will change everyone's way of thinking about gays and Lesbians.

I am not upset with TCF banks and Valley Fair only these are good examples of other places like the Mall of America, and most jewelry stores around the world controlled by men and most likely sex texting.

These men controllers are the Girl's boss. The Girls have to have his number to call in person to call in late, sick, or on vacation. The Girls need his number in their cell phones. They could block or erase the number they do this after they quit.

When I was in the nut house I called around 30 government offices and politely ask them to go to the TCF bank and break a 20 into 5s so just ask the bank teller to do this for you but when they got there are no bank tellers in that bank. Hard to believe but that man controlling the girl with sex the girls just stood there with nothing to do. Just so that bad man could see the girl's just fine. He will no longer be able to do this much longer until this book is released.

To understand Orbs better look at front cover of book see the Orb then Google Orbs.

SHE IS STRAIGHT

I find that when I sit patiently and watch people, if I or we as normal human beings wanted to, I or we could hand a piece of paper to each person to let them know if they are gay, lesbian, or Straight. This is the interesting thing– as soon as children can walk we can tell if they are gay or lesbian or Straight. This will sound alarming but you find it is true over time.

This is a good time to cry as we feel sorry for Lesbians and gays it is good for our eyes!!!!

I've learned a lot from observing people, but I implore you to also observe the people around you. Any Straight person can observe the people around them and figure out the sexuality of people under 30 based on how they look at you. If they turn their heads and look you Straight in the eyes, they're Straight people trying to learn from you. Try observing the people around you the next time you're at café or a mall and see what you learn from them.

When we first moved to this house I found a photo in a book of a rainbow and had my step daughter Goldie help me paint the bridge. We drew lines on it with a pencil, she sat on the ground as I painted the bridge in the order she told me to. After the bridge was painted we realized the colors were backwards. The moral of this story is we all make mistakes.

I think gays or Lesbians can try a new way of advertising their sexual preferences by a ring on their finger, **blue for gay men** and **pink for lesbian women**.

After you read this book people will understand this book will control the world's population by understanding who are Lesbians or gays.

From an analytical stand point there are 33% Straight, 33% Lesbians and 33% gays on planet earth.

Someday I would like to go to the mega mall and hand out a small piece of paper with a G, or L to and give it to the parents so they will know.

Gays and Lesbians have feelings for each other just by watching people for example; for some reason Lesbians feel more conferrable talking to other Girl's or woman rather than men. I learned by watching people in the nuthouse for 3 weeks.

Lesbians might lay in bed together more comfortably without sex they are perfectly happy they are just born this way and understand each other because they are Girls this is true with gay men.

There was once a photo that implied Goldie is a lesbian on her face book the one that upset me. When you look at your children's eyes you will know what their sexual preferences are when they are under the age of 14 years old. Over time they will change because of what you have learned from this book.

I am retired at 64 years old on a fixed income.

In the psychiatrist office I could not believe what I witnessed that is everyone in the waiting room was fat; probably from the sleeping drugs they are giving us. If we sleep to much we most likely do not get enough exercise. The older girls could have been young hookers at one time.

The thing that I wonder men if caught with trying to hook up with a hooker or prostitute and to find out it is a cop that unhappy man goes to jail for years leaving his wife and children at home and the hooker gets the nut house then the doctors get them fat.

The drugs they are giving me are affecting my testosterone level I am not attracted to Girls. However as soon as my contract is expired no more case worker no more psychiatrist no more drugs just ask your <u>Attorney General</u> if you do not believe me they have temperately castrated me!

I ask a group of workers nurses in the nut house that is on drugs lots of them got teary eyes on me in other words they were on drugs. One day a male nurse had a hard time restrain a man and did it the wrong way. I could see he was having a hard time with it. Later I ask a veteran worker how you can cope with people like us. He said "we have to be admitted in to the mental hospital as well". They put us on drugs just so we can cope.

In the hospital there are good things too! Like on the PA system they play a song called "Twinkle, Twinkle Little Star" when new born baby is born, and C-sections as well!

Carrie my son's sister started texting me the wrong way. She led me on with sex. Then she showed her cell phone to the police. Then the police came to my house and put me in the nut house again. But this time I told the nurses she started it by suggesting me to have sex with me. She led me on. Then they let me out after they did a full investigation with in 1 hour.

The point I am trying to make is Goldie can now get the bad men at TCF bank if they are texting her in a wrong way and put all of them in the nut house for a long time. I know you Girls can put men in the nuthouse if another Girl comes forward and complains to the police and shows her phone with the bad sex texting to them.

The bad men at TCF bank after the police can get his TCF company cell phone the police and Goldie can find others he is texting wrong. The next Girl can file another clam in 3 weeks they will go to the nut house in a rescue ambulance then under contract for six mounts put him in the nut house over and over for years or he can leave banking. The men in the bank have been doing this for over six years and the police know all about it I told them the boss is controlling the Girls with sex, however they do not know what to do until now happy me!

After you get rid of the bad ones replace them with Girls or some other man and worn him this could happen to you as well. Did Goldie have sex with them we will never know?

I unfortunately had to kick Goldie my step daughter out of our house for fighting with my wife. My wife told me it was because she drank too much. The reason I did not know the reason, was because they were talking in a different language call tegalogo, Philippines.

If you kick out a son or daughter out of your house, try to come in contact with them or hopefully they could back to you and say hi.

Around 6 years ago I saw Goldie's face book and did not like what I saw. She was implying she was a lesbian and used Ronia's face on her Face book so dumb people like me had a hard time figuring it all out. Ronia is Goldie best lesbian friend! I heard on the radio at the time an employer is going to hire a new or old person they will look them up on face book. This told employers will look at peoples face book. I was unhappy Goldie is a lesbian not knowing she was born this way. Over the last 6 years I have been researching gay lesbian and Straight sex.

After I saw Goldie's face book I started handing letters to TCF bank tellers unhappy thinking Goldie's boss was having lesbian sex with Goldie and her Straight friends not knowing her Straight friends were hurting their feelings.

I handed out around 6 letters to the bank tellers where she worked hoping Goldie and all her Girl friends bank tellers saw the letters, not her boss. Apparently her dumb boss saw them the letters were intended to get her boss drunk get him for drinking and driving or marry dumb him then divorce him so they could get rid of him. Goldie was so unhappy with me she sent a letter to her sister in the Philippines; her sister sent it to my wife all most killed me. But Goldie has to realize I was after her boss. Her boss would come out of this office and hide behind the police not wanting to face me because he was and still guilty when it comes to sex under his conditions.

Around 1 year latter TCF moved to the new location on 130th and Ceader and I decided to apologize to her old boss with a apologizing letter. But what I saw made me so unhappy I had to go home and cry for a long time because that dumb boss is controlling the Girls with sex and I have been sending letters to the governs office because of the bad Burnsville police and dumb Mayor. I have been sending letters to my Governor of Minnesota Timothy James Walz office letting them know what I am try to accomplish hoping he would send a copy to the Burnsville police apparently he did not. One subject was important and that is; the city of Burnsville is receiving way too much money for the rental clean up act. I was wondering where did millions of dollars go? Not wanting to go to city hall alone the fear of the police putting me back in the nut house.

The Burnsville police know about my web site because the name was on my car, my Sons car and Wife's car the signs on my car showed the public my web site and try to show on my site I am trying to get a book on the market called "World Population Control". Blessing in disguise the 1 year delay I can add more to this book and change the name to for Girls only, men will like it to the original title was "Synchronicity".

I was just pointing out that when we look at a photo of people the gays stand out as well as lesbians. This is why the police were unhappy with me. You see the rainbow bridge in my front yard was a sex symbol as well. The day I removed the rainbow bridge from my yard I saw one Burnsville police car roll his window down as he was traveling in a counter clockwise direction as soon as he past my house on a very hot day he rolled it up.

My free public defender told me after my contract is over no more case workers and no more psychiatrist no more drugs and there is **a real possibility the Governor Girls changed all hospital contracts to let us all wean our self's off of drugs too!!!** Or the contract was always this way a small hint of not having a case worker a physiatrist and no more poison drugs. I am the one that discovered what the drugs are doing to me hopefully temporary castrated me. They do not do this procedure anymore so they can do it with drugs.

Straight men and Straight Girls will have sex. Gay men will have sex with Girls. Lesbians will have sex with other Lesbians. Gay men will have sex with gay men. Everything will be the same except after gays and Lesbians read this book your eyes will be Straight, after everyone reads this book in the world all eyes will be Straight except children under the age of 13 years old we have to teach them when they are ready with your family members.

Four types of leaders should be learned to recognize Analytical, Driver, Amiable and Expressive (Google it).

I am Analytical that is why this book is so short unhappy me! On the other hand, I was born this way.

A short book will last a long time.

This book has looping characteristics as well first is there are no page numbers; BC is Before Christ was born and the bible was around there were no page numbers, you are better-off reading this book over from the start and this will not include electronic kindle Books, over and over!

Second characteristic front cover of book at first you will read Third look at front cover of book look for the Orb, over and over!

Third characteristic and last; end of book (Why the colors for front book) orbs move all around us the colors represent orbs. red on front and back like bible; purple a girl color; a priest wears black and white. over and over!

I went to a church and filled the empty water bottle with holy water. Then I sprinkled it on a dying person in the hospital then he died "unhappy us".

The TV show Judge Judy; in this show if the plaintive are guilty their eyes become teary eyed, Judge Judy pickup on this human characteristic this helps her decision making process in her brain.

Orbs move around 30 to 35 miles per hour. This can be proven some day as a new science like Antony Van Leeuwenhoek that discovers microorganisms. I will have 2 web-sites will reflect this someday.

Please this book needs to be a chain letter in all <u>middle school libraries</u> from grade schools to collages then all public libraries around the world with a target of ages 13 to 15 years old in schools. This book can be found at Barnes and Noble bookstore. You know anyone that wants this book for free just have them call the library on their cell phone and ask the librarian if they have it or have them parches it for the school librarian this will be handy for the sex class teacher.

Women or girls in churches of any denomination could buy lots of these books then sell them or just give them to members. Thanks

**It helps other families to identify each other with arrows and
labels to teach others who are Lesbian, gays or straights.**

My two web-sites coming soon!

POPBUBBLES.US

POPBUBBLE.US

Women like it when we men call them young Girls or you have pretty eyes!

We men like to be = called = young men.

Why do Girls put makeup on? They are trying to attract boys or men.

It is my hope the Governor of Minnesota will help me publish this book or help in advertising of our book. The sooner the book is published the sooner we men will not cry. The girls will put the bad texting men in the nut house. You see the governor is expecting me to keep him updated. So we will give him this book and hopefully his girls or men staff will call me with a publisher. The governor office can or my new publisher will call me soon.

It is our hope the Governor endorses this book someday.

We would like to meet Tim Walz at the Mediterranean Cruise Buffet and have photos of him and my book then put a photo of us, Tim and our book in the news paper. We want the Burnsville police commander and the mayor of Burnsville to be there as well. Thank you

ABOUT THE INVENTOR

When I was around four years old my mom told me a story; my neighbors got mad at me for– well let me put to you this way– when my neighbor went into his house for lunch after painting his house, he left the can of oil based paint and brush in fount of his open garage door. So I got the can and brush and painted the inside of his garage.

I have always been an inventor type of person since I was a young child. When I was in fourth grade I found a television set in an empty lot that was under development for a housing project. I asked my mom if I could take it. My mom asked why I wanted it. I told her I wanted to figure out how it works. So she helped me load the television into our station wagon and brought it home. Then I started taking it apart. This was the start of my fun inventing adventure that has lasted throughout my life.

When I was in the sixth grade I built an airplane using a Cox .049 engine the airplane had two wires attached to it so I could fly it around in a circle until I got dizzy. I would then try to flip it over so I could fly it in the other direction but that is when I always crashed it. I then had to fix it. In the winter I used the same motor, a Cox .049, and built an air sled that had two skis with no control strings so it would crash and then I'd have to fix it.

After I finished two years of college I wanted to build a robot– so I did. The total cost was around ten thousand dollars. When I built it my main intention was to learn more about how they work and I was hoping to display it as a tool to attract a crowd to promote a product. I built it with old technology so I could use used parts that were going obsolete. I used a programmable logic controller with about one thousand wires. I gave it the name Dino the dinosaur because it was built with old technology.

Dino could see players and talk to them. A person controlled it in another room. Dino could deal out cards to seven players, pick up the cards, and hand out a prize to the winner. Finally, he could pick up all the cards and shuffle them. It took Dino about fifteen minutes for each game.

I did try to patent it but Mark, my patent attorney, thought it would be very expensive because of all the moving parts. I did have it on display at the Savage library for one public showing. It can be seen on YouTube– the video is called card playing robot. Because I could not come up with a sponsor for funding it just sat around in my shed for years and eventually I had to dismantle it. But it did help when I was looking for work interviewers could see it on YouTube.

I also invented a Lotion warmer. It is different than all the competition. It was a ceramic container with a ceramic lid. I put electric heaters and thermostat in the bottom and developed a way to circulate the heat. All a person needed to do was plug it in, put a plastic container inside it, and cover it. Then all they had to do was either remove it from the container or pump the Lotion in the container. Unfortunately, I lost interest in it and the partner I was working with died.

I also invented something I called gutter flowers. It was a self-contained container with a nylon sock filled with soil and peat moss. I had all my gutters filled with flowers. The gutter flowers had a good design for rainfall. All someone needed to do was put a flower in the gutter flower container and put it in their gutter. When it came time to water them, just spray your roof with water. My patent attorney Mark did not think it was a good idea because everyone would want to sue me for water damage in their basements even though my gutter flowers did not cause the damage. Because Mark recommended I should not patent this idea, I felt he really wanted to help me. I think there are a lot of Patent Attorneys that would have patented the gutter flower idea knowing there would be lawsuits or simply overlooked this important thought. This is why I know Mark is what I call an honest Patent Attorney.

Finally, I invented a vacuum poring station. This invention would suck up corn with a hose and fill the vacuum cleaner. Then all a person had to do was pull a lever and the corn would fall into a five gallon bucket in the bottom of the vacuum cleaner container to give up on that idea. I did patent it with a provisional patent but when the price of corn jumped up to seven dollars a bushel it was cheaper to burn natural gas.

ABOUT THE AUTHOR

Chuck Simon is 65 years old and is retired. He has been writing books for 5 years now. He is excited to publish one of his best written book.

ABOUT THE BOOK:

All women and girls will learn how to prevent your boss from controlling you with sex. Your boss needs your **Cell Phone** number in case you call in sick or he wants to talk. He can start texting you the wrong way called sex texting. This can be prevented. Show your cell phone to the police then see what happens next.

Please this book needs to be a chain letter in all <u>middle school libraries</u> from grade schools to collages then all public libraries around the world with a target of ages 13 to 15 years old in schools. You know anyone that wants this book for free just have them call the public library on their cell phone and ask the librarian if they have it or have them parches it for the school librarian this will be handy for the sex class teacher this fall. The librarian will read it then she can help advertise for us.

Thanks

The First Advent

Stories and Activities

MICHAEL J. LARSON

Illustrations by Janine Ringdahl Schmidt

WESTBOW
PRESS®
A DIVISION OF THOMAS NELSON
& ZONDERVAN

Scripture texts, prefaces, introductions, footnotes and cross references used in this work are taken from the New American Bible, revised edition © 2010, 1991, 1986, 1970 Confraternity of Christian Doctrine, Inc., Washington, DC All Rights Reserved. No part of this work may be reproduced or transmitted in any form or by any means, electronic or mechanical, including photocopying, recording, or by any information storage and retrieval system, without permission in writing from the copyright owner.

WestBow Press books may be ordered through booksellers or by contacting:

WestBow Press
A Division of Thomas Nelson & Zondervan
1663 Liberty Drive
Bloomington, IN 47403
www.westbowpress.com
1 (866) 928-1240

Because of the dynamic nature of the Internet, any web addresses or links contained in this book may have changed since publication and may no longer be valid. The views expressed in this work are solely those of the author and do not necessarily reflect the views of the publisher, and the publisher hereby disclaims any responsibility for them.

Any people depicted in stock imagery provided by Getty Images are models, and such images are being used for illustrative purposes only. Certain stock imagery © Getty Images.

ISBN: 978-1-9736-2552-0 (sc)
ISBN: 978-1-9736-2555-1 (e)

Library of Congress Control Number: 2018904245

Print information available on the last page.

WestBow Press rev. date: 04/13/2018

To Priudence Ramos, whose suggestion about a need for Advent stories for children inspired the author to create *The First Advent*.

Contents

Introduction

Hi, kids! We call the four weeks before Christmas Advent. During these four weeks, we wait and prepare our hearts for the arrival of Baby Jesus.

This book will help you do that, as it contains a reading or activity for each day of Advent. Complete the assignment each day and discover how animals and a couple of stable workers prepared the stable and their hearts for the arrival of Baby Jesus.

Upon the completion of this book, it is the author's wish that you will be able to welcome Baby Jesus into your heart on Christmas morning.

The author gives your caregivers permission to make copies of the activity pages so each of you will have your own page to complete.

Happy Advent!

November 30—A Visit from Andrew the Angel

The old stable stood on the edge of Bethlehem. It was built against a wall of rock. The mouth of a cave opened in the back of the stable, and the cave offered an overflow space for the stable's livestock.

It was dusk, and the animals were quiet. Sleep would soon be overtaking many of them. However, Roger Rat and his pals were just waking up and preparing to search for a snack of grain.

Suddenly the darkened stable was filled with a bright light. In the center of the light stood a huge figure. Over eight feet tall and wearing a scarlet robe, the figure smiled with kind eyes.

"Attention, animals of the stable. I am Andrew the angel. I have come from heaven with important news."

The stable animals stared wide-eyed at the enormous figure.

Andrew continued, "In twenty-five days, God's own Son will be born in this stable. He will be named Jesus and is destined to become the Savior of the world. His mother's name is Mary, and His earthly father is named Joseph."

Together, the animals of the stable murmured, "Baby Jesus, God's own Son. Wow!"

"Use the next days wisely to prepare the stable for the arrival of heaven's royalty, Baby Jesus."

The cow, whose name was Cow, stared up at Andrew as she asked, "We are living in a dusty, smelly stable. How can we make it a worthy place for a king to be born?"

"You all have your gifts. Take some time and think. I'm sure each one of you will come up with a way to prepare the stable for the arrival of Baby Jesus."

With that, the bright light dimmed, and the angel was gone.

Darkness returned to the stable. However, it took several hours for calm to return. The excited animals discussed the assignment Andrew had given them to make the stable a worthy place for the birth of the King of the world.

But now the animals faced a difficult task. Each animal had to determine what gift they were going to give to Baby Jesus.

If you were living in the stable awaiting the arrival of Baby Jesus, what gift would you give?

December 1—Cow Can't Think of a Gift

The rising sun sent beams of sunlight through the cracks in the stable wall.

Cow moaned, "I didn't get much sleep last night."

"What's bothering you?" cooed the pigeon.

"What gift do I have to help prepare the stable for the arrival of Baby Jesus?"

Roger Rat overheard Cow as he was scurrying back to his home under a hay pile. "You've got lots of time to figure that out," he said as he disappeared into the opening to his home.

"Twenty-four days is not very long," Cow said. "Especially when I don't have any idea at all."

The pigeon replied, "Oh, Cow, your gift should be an easy one. Every morning and evening after you are milked, give Mary and Joseph a mug of warm milk."

"Even though I produce the milk, the innkeeper uses the milk to make butter and cheese to sell to the people staying at his inn," Cow said. "He would not be happy if I gave away milk that he could have sold to his customers."

"I suppose you are right, but what a nice gift it would have made for Mary and Joseph," the pigeon said.

"If I did give Mary and Joseph milk and the innkeeper found out, my name would get changed really fast. I wouldn't be Cow anymore."

"What would your new name be?" the pigeon asked.

"I'm afraid I would be referred to as hamburger!" Cow said.

"Yikes! We don't want you to become hamburger! Maybe we better think of a more suitable gift to give."

Both the pigeon and Cow nodded in agreement.

Then Roger Rat stuck his head out of his hole and said, "Say a prayer to God and ask him for wisdom about a gift. He will help you, I'm sure."

Cow grabbed a mouthful of hay from her manger and chewed for a few minutes as she thought about Roger Rat's suggestion. "Say a prayer. What a great idea. Why didn't I think of that? Okay, a prayer it will be."

Boys and girls, God always answers prayers, although we don't always like the answer. What do you think His prayer answer will be for Cow?

December 2–A Prayer Is Answered

The sun had set, and the evening milking was finished. Cow had her head down in the manger gobbling up some grain when Roger Rat scurried up to her.

"Can I share some of your grain? Can I … can I?"

"Of course, you can," answered Cow. "Don't I always share my grain with you?"

"Thank you, thank you! Has God answered your prayer? Do you know what gift you will give?"

"Not yet," said Cow. "But I must be patient. I have twenty-three days before I have to make that decision."

"God will drop an idea on you by that time I am sure," replied Roger.

At that very moment, the stableman dropped a large bundle of hay into the manger. The hay landed on top of Roger.

"Who turned out the light? Help me, help me!" Roger said.

"Don't panic, Roger. I'll save you." Using her head, Cow butted the pile of hay, and as it rolled, Roger got tangled up in the strands of hay.

"Now I'm all tangled up! Untangle me! Untangle me please!"

Cow gently used her nose to push the hay around in the manger. But the more she pushed, the more tangled Roger became.

"I might be trapped for life!"

"Don't be silly," cooed the pigeon as she and several other pigeons flew into the manger and began pecking and scratching at the twisted strands of hay. In seconds, Roger Rat was free.

"Oh, thank you! You all saved my life!"

Cow continued butting the pile of hay again and again. "Umm, very interesting," Cow said.

"What's so interesting?" questioned Roger Rat.

"This hay is soft and would make a wonderful bed."

"There wouldn't be room for you though, Cow. You are way too big."

"Not for me, silly. For Baby Jesus. That will be my gift."

"Your prayer has been answered!" squealed the rat.

"Yes, it has. My gift to Baby Jesus will be my manger for his bed."

December 3-A Spider Gift

Two barn spiders, Burt and Barb, had been spinning webs above the cow's manger for several months.

The flies were abundant in the stable, so it was a good place to catch their breakfast, lunch, dinner, and occasionally a midnight snack.

Burt and Barb were suspended high above the manger, resting on a newly spun web, when Burt said, "Cow has decided to give Baby Jesus her manger for a bed. What can we do to welcome Baby Jesus?"

"I've been thinking about that. We need to make the gift something special," Barb said.

"Andrew says we should use our gifts, and spinning webs is what we are good at," said Burt.

"You're right. How could we use spinning webs to honor Baby Jesus?"

Both spiders were silent for a long time until Barb said, "I have an idea." But because she wanted it to be a surprise, she whispered her idea to Burt.

"That's a cool idea. Let's get started on it right away."

So the pair of spiders began spinning. But because they were spinning a web unlike any web they had ever spun before, they made mistakes and had to do parts over. Also, the web was very fragile. The web strands broke and had to be repaired.

"Oh, I hope we can get this done before Baby Jesus arrives," sighed Barb.

"We can, and we will!" Burt said.

It sounds like Burt and Barb have a big job on their hands. We'll check back in a few days and see how they are coming along. I wonder what kind of special web they will be spinning.

If you were Burt and Barb, what kind of special web would you spin?

December 4–A Gift from the Stable Boy

David was the stable boy. His job was to care for the animals in the stable. He fed them and watered them. Sometimes he had to exercise some of the animals, which he really enjoyed.

Many travelers who stayed at the Bethlehem Inn kept their animals at the stable. Camels, oxen, and donkeys kept David very busy, but David didn't mind because he loved all animals. Even Roger Rat was his friend.

After Andrew the angel had visited the stable, David tried to decide what he could do to prepare for the arrival of Baby Jesus.

The place is kind of drab. There must be something I can do to brighten things up, he thought.

When he had his chores done, he went for walks out in the country. As he walked, he thought of ways to decorate the stable.

One afternoon as he was trudging along, he spotted a cedar tree. It was tall, slender, and perfectly shaped. Its dark green foliage added to its majesty.

"Now there's a tree fit for a king," murmured David.

He ran back to the stable and searched the tool room until he found an ax. After chopping the tree down, David dragged the cedar to the stable, placed it in a stand, and stood it next to the manger.

"It needs a little something more."

In the meantime, Roger Rat had been searching for a snack of grain in the manger. He stuck his head up and said, "Baby Jesus is going to be a king, and a king needs a crown, so put a crown on top of the tree."

"Good idea," cheered David, and he raced to the storage room. There he found a discarded strip of leather. Using a knife, he fashioned a crown and decorated it with shiny stones that he found on the edge of the dusty road.

Roger Rat grabbed the crown. He scurried to the top of the tree and placed the crown on the top branch.

"Ah, a tree fit for a king," cheered Roger Rat.

"Especially a baby king destined to save the world," added David.

Michael J. Larson

December 5-Surprise Decorations

David rose early to care for the animals in the stable. He was giving the animals their rations of grain.

As he approached Cow's manger, he murmured, "That's right. Cow doesn't eat here anymore. Baby Jesus will be sleeping here soon."

He stopped to admire the cedar tree and its crown when he gasped, "My goodness, what have we here? Someone has added more decorations to the tree!"

The tree was decorated with a colorful garland that started low on the tree and wound round and round the tree until finally reaching the top. The garland was made of interwoven strands of red, gold, blue, green, and white cloth.

Also, scattered over the branches were colorful cloth bows.

"The tree is even more beautiful!" exclaimed David. "But who could have done such a thing?"

Roger Rat had heard David rattling the feed bucket and had come looking for a free breakfast. Overhearing David, he replied, "I don't know who is responsible, but I'm going to find out."

"You do that, Roger Rat, and let me know what you discover."

Later in the day, Roger Rat's voice echoed through the stable. "David, where are you? I've got something to show you."

"Over here," answered David as he busily spread fresh straw under a pair of oxen.

Looking up, David observed an unusual sight. Roger Rat came marching down the center aisle of the stable, and behind him marched fifteen nervous mice.

"Meet the tree decorators. They are a little nervous because they aren't used to being out in the open like this."

"Where did they get the decorations?" asked David.

One of the mice spoke up. "We went to the fabric shop in town and gathered up the cloth scraps that were going to be thrown out."

A second mouse continued, "We wanted to do something special for Baby Jesus but didn't want to scare Mary and Joseph. Many people are scared of us mice, so we did our decorating late at night."

"Well, thank you, mice, for making our tree even more beautiful," said David. "Now hurry back to your homes before the stable cat discovers you."

"We forgot about the cat!" screamed the mice in unison. You have never seen fifteen mice move so fast!

December 6–A Time to Color

Today we are going to take a break from reading and do a little coloring. Get your crayons or colored pencils and color the picture of David and Roger Rat on the next page.

They are admiring the decorated cedar tree. Do you see any mice in the picture?

December 7—A Gift of Silence

Tuffy the rooster ruled the stable. His head was adorned with a huge red comb and red waddles. His plume of red and black tail feathers made him appear larger than he really was.

During the day, Tuffy escorted his hens into the fields surrounding the stable, where they would scratch and search for juicy bugs and plant seeds.

Tuffy had one job that he was very proud of. Every morning, starting at five o'clock, Tuffy flew to the top of a large fence post, craned his neck, and sounded off, "Cock-a-doodle-do!" Not once, not twice but many times for the next several hours.

Tuffy was very proud of being the stable's alarm clock.

The flock of chickens was present when Andrew the angel made his visit, so they too were trying to decide what gift they might add to honor the birth of the Christ child. Many ideas were discussed, but nothing was agreed upon.

Early one morning, the hens were roosting high in the stable rafters when the air was filled with "Cock-a-doodle-do!"

"Sounds like Tuffy the rooster is announcing another day," said one of the hens, yawning.

A second hen said, "When Baby Jesus arrives, that cock-a-doodle-doing is going to be very disturbing. Not only for Baby Jesus but also for Mary and Joseph."

Suddenly one of the hens asked, "Are all of you hens thinking what I'm thinking?"

In unison, the hens cried, "Yes, our gift will be for Tuffy to give up his noisy crowing in the mornings."

"For as long as Baby Jesus is in the stable," said one of the hens.

The excited hens flew down from their roosts in the rafters and ran in search of Tuffy to bring him the news.

At first, Tuffy did not like the idea of turning off his cock-a-doodle-do. He enjoyed being the stable's alarm clock.

The hens reminded Tuffy that Baby Jesus had come to bring God's love and save us from our sins. He was the Savior of the world.

"I suppose for such an important little baby, I could close my beak for a few mornings," muttered Tuffy.

The hens cheered and flapped their wings with excitement. They were happy the mornings would be peaceful for the sleeping babe. In fact, all the animals in the stable were looking forward to no cock-a-doodle-dos in the morning.

What a wonderful gift, the gift of silence.

December 8-One Hump Needs Gift Help

The camel, nicknamed One Hump, was contentedly chewing a mouthful of hay when Roger Rat approached.

"Hey, One Hump, what will be your gift for Baby Jesus?"

One Hump frowned and continued to chew for several minutes. Finally, he said, "I've thought and thought, and I just can't think of a gift. I could give Baby Jesus a ride, but he will be too young for that."

"You are good at giving rides and carrying supplies," agreed Roger Rat. "But they won't qualify as a gift."

"I know."

"What's something else you do well?"

"I spit really well. We camels are known for that."

"No, no, yuck! Anything else?"

"I'm a camel with very few talents."

"Maybe I can help."

"Who said that?" gasped Roger Rat.

Turning around, Roger Rat looked upward and viewed Andrew the angel's face smiling down at him.

"Hi, Andrew. We need to help One Hump figure out a gift to give Baby Jesus."

Andrew replied, "One Hump's gift will be needed when the three wise men (magi) come to visit the baby. They will bring gifts of gold, frankincense, and myrrh."

Puzzled, One Hump asked, "Andrew, what gift will I give?"

"The wise men will have traveled a great distance. It will be much too far for them to walk, so they will be riding camels."

"Camels!" shouted One Hump. "Heck, I know a few things about camels, since I am one."

"Yes, you are." Roger Rat grinned. "Does that give you a gift idea?"

"I better brush up on becoming a camel host because my gift will be to entertain the camels while the wise men are offering homage to Baby Jesus."

"Yea! You can swap camel stories with them," added Roger Rat.

One Hump smiled and went back to chewing on some hay. "Now that I know what my gift will be, I gotta keep my energy up. Entertaining visiting camels takes a lot of energy, and I'd better brush up on some good camel stories too."

December 9–A Gift from the Flock

Fuzzy and Wooly, two sheep, were grazing together on a hillside overlooking the stable.

"Wooly, what is your special gift?" questioned Fuzzy.

"You mean a gift like Andrew the angel talked about?"

"Yes, that's exactly what I mean."

Wooly nibbled on some blades of grass for several seconds before replying. "I've been thinking about my gifts ever since Andrew talked about them. I have the nicest b-a-a-a in the flock."

"Maybe you could sing Baby Jesus a song."

"I could do that. I know that old nursery rhyme sheep song."

"What song is that?"

In her finest sheep voice, Wooly sang, "Baa, baa, black sheep, have you any wool? Yes, sir, yes, sir, three bags full. One for my master, one for the dame, and one for the little boy who lives down the lane."

"That is a nice song, and you sang it beautifully, but it doesn't fit the occasion," said Fuzzy. "Remember that Baby Jesus has come to save the world."

"We could change the words to fit the occasion," Wooly said.

"And what would that sound like?"

Wooly was thoughtful for a few minutes. Then a smile filled her face as she sang, "Baa, baa,

black sheep, have you any wool? Yes, sir, yes, sir, three bags full. One for my master, one for the dame, and one for the babe who in the stable just came."

By this time, the whole flock of sheep had gathered around Wooly and Fuzzy. All the sheep nodded in agreement that the new rhyme was much more meaningful. But would it really be a worthwhile gift?

The members of the flock were discussing this very topic when suddenly Fuzzy exclaimed, "I know what our gift will be! The rhyme tells us, if we'd only listen."

Together, the sheep recited the first line, "Baa, baa, black sheep, have you any wool?"

Then the flock cried in unison, "Wool! We all have wool! That will be our gift."

The sheep were happy to gift their wool to Baby Jesus. But the wool was attached to the sheep. That was a problem that had to be solved. The wool couldn't be given away when it was still attached.

But now it's your bedtime, so we'll have to wait until tomorrow to see how the sheep solve the wool problem. Good night!

Oh, one more thing. If you have trouble falling asleep

tonight, try counting sheep. Remember first Wooly, then Fuzzy, and then the rest of the flock one sheep at a time. Sleep tight.

December 10–Shearing Solves the Problem

Remember last night's reading when each of the sheep agreed to donate some of their wool to Baby Jesus? But you readers were reminded that the wool was still attached to the sheep. That was a big problem … until one of the sheep in the flock spoke up.

"I overheard the shepherds talking. They said that next week we would all be sheared."

"Then we will each donate a handful of wool to Baby Jesus," said Wooly.

Now, Anna was the stable's milkmaid. She came in the morning and evenings to milk Cow. But she was also able to spin wool into threads and make yarn.

So, the next morning as Anna left the stable with a fresh container of milk, she was surrounded by the flock of sheep.

"Anna, can you please help us?" said Fuzzy.

Anna listened politely as the sheep explained their problem.

"Oh, I'm so glad you came to see me," replied Anna. "I was wondering what gift I could give the baby too."

"Now we each will give a gift. We will provide the wool," squealed Fuzzy.

"And I'll spin the wool into yarn and make a special gift for Baby Jesus," said Anna. "I'll have to think about what to make with the wool."

"Do tell us when you decide," said Fuzzy. "It must be a special gift."

"I will have to think of a very special gift, but when I do, I won't tell you what it is until the gift is complete. It will be a surprise."

The sheep moaned and groaned. They wanted to know what the gift would be at that very moment.

Finally, Wooly said, "Okay, a surprise it will be—but hurry. We can't wait to see what you turn our gifts of wool into."

What do you think Anna the milkmaid will make with the sheep's wool? Everyone take a guess, and we'll find out during tomorrow's reading if anyone is right.

December 11—A Gift Made from Wool

For the next week, the sheep greeted Anna every morning and evening.

The sheep looked different. Their long, wool coats, some dirty and weed infested, had been sheared. The removal of the old wool exposed clean, close-cropped wool that left the sheep looking neat and trim.

Roger Rat commented, "You sheep look really sharp after being sheared. I should have had them shear me too."

"Baa-d idea," replied one of the sheep. "There's not a big market for rat hair."

All the sheep chuckled, while Roger Rat blushed.

Anna walked by carrying a pail of fresh, warm milk and overheard Roger's conversation with the sheep.

"Sorry, Roger. I don't think your rat hair would have made very good yarn. Anyway, the gift is almost ready. I'll be able to show it to you tomorrow when I come to milk Cow."

"Yeah!" cheered Roger, and the sheep bleated with excitement too.

"I wonder what Anna made with our wool!"

The flock was so excited no one could get to sleep until the wee hours of the morning.

Finally, the sun began to peek over the horizon—morning at last! The flock of sheep gathered around Cow as they anxiously waited for the arrival of Anna.

The clank of a pail sounded as Anna entered the stable.

"Okay, sheep, back away from Cow," said Anna. "I'll need some room to milk her."

Roger Rat was sitting on the back of one of the sheep as he said, "Did you bring Baby Jesus's gift made from wool?"

"I'll get it after milking is complete. We must not get it dirty."

The sheep milled around aimlessly as Anna milked Cow. Finally, the milking was complete. Anna stood up holding the pail of warm milk.

"Follow me," she instructed as she walked to the stable door, where she had laid her cloak on a pile of straw. Next to her cloak was a package.

Anna unwrapped the package and held up a beautiful blanket.

A murmur of approval spread through the flock.

"It is beautiful!" exclaimed Roger Rat. "And you have a picture of an angel in the middle of the blanket."

"Even Baby Jesus needs a guardian angel," replied Anna.

Each member of the flock thanked Anna for turning their wool into such a beautiful gift.

Now they could hardly wait for the arrival of the baby king.

December 12–Picture-Coloring Time

It's coloring time again. Get those crayons and colored pencils and color some of the stable animals in the drawing on the next page.

December 13—A Very Late Gift

Dan the Donkey was depressed. He had heard Andrew the angel say that Mary and Joseph would be traveling to Bethlehem on a donkey. That meant he would have to compete with another donkey if he wanted to give Baby Jesus a gift.

Dan lived in the stable. The innkeeper used Dan to haul supplies of hay and grain to the stable for the animals staying there. Sometimes he carried trunks and baggage for some of the inn's guests. Hauling supplies was his talent, but Mary and Joseph's donkey had the same talent.

"That other donkey has been carrying Mary and Baby Jesus all the way from Nazareth, and all I've done is carry a few sacks of grain and a little hay." Dan sighed.

Roger Rat and Cow consoled the donkey.

"We all have special jobs to do, and we appreciate the hay and grain you deliver," said Cow.

"Thanks for saying that," murmured Dan.

"I have a thought," said Cow. "Some of the sheep thought about singing a song to Baby Jesus but decided a gift of wool would be better. Maybe you could sing a donkey song for the babe."

"I'm not sure how good of a singer I am, but I could give it a try, I suppose." With that, Dan opened his mouth, and out came the most horrible-sounding "Hee-haw, hee-haw."

It was so bad that some of the animals close to Dan had to plug their ears.

"Let's scratch that idea. Instead, let's call a meeting of the stable animals and brainstorm what Dan's gift should be," suggested Roger Rat.

All the stable animals cheered in agreement as they gathered around Dan the donkey.

But before any suggestions could be made, a bright light burst forth next to Dan, and there in the middle of the light stood Andrew the angel.

Roger Rat exclaimed, "Boy, are we glad to see you, Andrew! We have a problem."

"You need to know what Dan the donkey's talent and gift will be," said Andrew.

"How did you know that?" gasped Roger.

"Because, Roger, he's an angel. Remember?" said Cow. "Angels know those things."

"Your gift, Dan, is going to be very special," stated Andrew. "But it is going to be thirty-three years late."

All the stable animals gasped in shock. Everyone began talking all at once. "What did Andrew mean? How could a gift be thirty-three years late?"

What do you think Andrew meant by that statement? We're going to have to wait until tomorrow night to find out because it's bedtime. In fact, if Dan the donkey could say something right now, he would say, "Hee-hee-haw!" which is donkey talk for "Sweet dreams!"

I wonder what the thirty-three-year-late gift could be …

December 14—Grandpa Dan

In last night's reading, Andrew had just told Dan the donkey that his gift to Baby Jesus would be thirty-three years late. The stable animals were confused and were all talking at one time.

"None of us will even be alive in thirty-three years, so how will Jesus receive Dan's gift?" asked Cow.

"Who will be around to give Him the gift?" questioned Roger the Rat.

The stable animals were coming up with ideas for how to handle a thirty-three-year-late gift, but no one could come up with an idea that made any sense.

Attempting to calm the animals, Andrew raised his hand to get their attention. Then he explained, "When Baby Jesus grows up—in fact, he will be thirty-three years old—he will be preparing to enter the city of Jerusalem as a hero of the people."

Jesus will say, "Go into the village opposite
you, and as you enter it you will find a colt
tethered on which no one had ever sat.
Untie it and bring it here." (Lk. 19:30)

The animals stared at Andrew in amazement. The baby was not yet born, and Andrew was prophesying what He would say and do thirty-three years in the future!

Andrew continued, "The colt Jesus will speak about is a baby donkey. And the baby donkey, Dan, will be your gift to Baby Jesus thirty-three years late."

"But I don't understand," sputtered Dan the donkey. "How could that baby donkey be a gift from me?"

"Because that colt will be your grandson, and he will carry Jesus into Jerusalem."

"I'm going to be a grandpa!" Dan beamed. "What an honor for my family to carry the king of the world into Jerusalem."

All the stable animals cheered for Dan the donkey. How special his gift would be, even thirty-three years late. Thirty-three years late but right on time.

Dan was pretty excited about his thirty-three-year-late gift, and for the next few weeks, he walked around the stable proudly wearing a big donkey grin.

December 15–A Gift from Roger Rat

Roger Rat came scurrying down the stable aisle. Anna had just completed the evening milking. Seeing Roger, she said, "Did you like my sewing job on your gift for Baby Jesus?"

Cow was chewing her cud and gazed at Roger as he approached. "What gift would that be, Roger?" Cow asked. "I thought the only talent you had was searching for kernels of grain late at night."

Roger Rat grinned at Cow and said, "I'm a feather finder."

Then he turned to Anna and replied, "Oh, you did a wonderful job. I am sure Baby Jesus will love it."

"Feather finder?" questioned Cow. "How do you use that talent?"

"I keep my eyes open for feathers—chicken feathers, sparrow feathers, pigeon feathers, or dove feathers. Actually, any kind of feather I find lying around the stable will do. When I find them, I store them in my tunnel under the hay pile. I have been doing this ever since Andrew the angel told us about the upcoming birth of Baby Jesus."

"You are going to give Baby Jesus a pile of feathers for His birthday?" asked Cow.

"Not exactly, but just give me a minute, and I'll show you."

Roger Rat scampered to the hole in the hay pile and disappeared.

Within minutes, something white immerged from the hole. Roger's pointed nose, whiskers, and tiny, beady eyes were visible under a beautiful white pillow that rested on Roger's back.

"What a beautiful feather pillow!" cried Cow. "That's why you were collecting feathers."

"Anna sewed a pillow case to put the feathers in. Come feel how soft it is."

Roger Rat proudly paraded the beautiful, little pillow around the stable for all to see. The animals were impressed with Roger Rat's special gift.

"Now, Roger Rat," said Anna, "you better return that pillow to your hay tunnel so it stays clean. Baby Jesus needs a clean pillow to rest His head on."

As Roger Rat and his feather-filled pillow disappeared into Roger's home, Cow said, "I can't wait for the arrival of the little baby."

All the stable animals excitedly agreed and were hopeful that their gifts would be well received.

December 16–Roger Rat Puzzle

On the following page is a picture of Roger Rat and his pillow. There is a problem, however, as the artist got the picture a little scrambled.

Cut the squares out and reassemble the picture so that Roger Rat and his pillow are visible.

Then glue the puzzle squares on a second sheet of paper and hang the resulting picture of Roger Rat and his pillow on your bedroom wall.

Happy cutting and pasting!

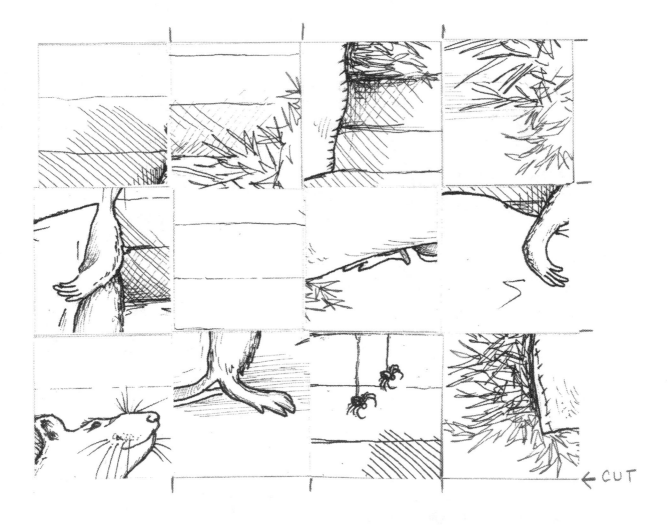

December 17–A Gift from the Pigeons

The pigeons were just settling onto their roosts high up in the stable rafters.

Penelope was the oldest pigeon, so she assigned herself the job of being the pigeon boss. All the other pigeons liked Penelope, so they accepted her bossy ways and looked to her as their leader.

"We need to decide on a gift for the Christ Child," stated Penelope.

"Roger Rat used some of our feathers to make a tiny pillow," responded one of the roosting birds.

Another pigeon added, "The pillow is a mixture of all kinds of bird feathers, not just ours."

"That's why we need to give a gift that comes just from us. It's late, but let's think about a possible gift and share some ideas tomorrow," replied Penelope.

So, the birds settled onto their roosts and thought of possible gifts. Soon they were all fast asleep.

Tuffy's early-morning crowing awakened the pigeons. They fluffed their feathers and flapped their wings as they prepared to leave their roosts.

Hopefully, David spilled a little grain as he fed the livestock. Spilled grain makes a wonderful breakfast for the pigeons.

Before they flew off in search of breakfast, Penelope said, "Does anyone have a gift idea for the Baby Jesus?"

The pigeons visited among themselves, but no one could come up with any good ideas.

As David finished feeding the animals, he overheard the pigeons' discussion in the rafters above his head.

"I know what gift you pigeons can give Baby Jesus," he said.

The pigeons peered down at David and in one voice said, "Tell us, David! Please tell us!"

"I'm going to put this feed sack in the grain bin, and I'll be right back and tell you my idea."

As David walked away, the pigeons visited excitedly.

What was the gift? Would it be a gift worthy for a baby destined to become king of the world?

Stay tuned because in tomorrow's reading, we will find out what gift David is thinking about.

In the meantime, what do you think that gift will be?

December 18-Celebrate with Song

In our last reading, the pigeons were waiting for David to return and share his gift idea for Baby Jesus.

When David didn't return, the pigeons flew down from the stable rafters and started pecking through the stable straw. Penelope said, "What's taking David so long to return? We want to know his gift idea."

"I can't wait to hear his idea," added one of the pigeons.

All the birds nodded in agreement.

"I think he's coming," whispered one of the birds.

As David strode into the stable, the birds gathered around him.

"Tell us your gift idea," pleaded the pigeons.

"First, I want to ask each of you to do something for me," replied David.

"What might that be?"

"I hear you all from time to time making a cooing sound when you're resting in the rafters. Sometimes the cooing becomes more like a warble."

"That's our pigeon language when we are relaxing," Penelope said.

"I know. I want to hear you all, one at a time, give me your best coo and warble."

So, each of the pigeons auditioned for David. Some cooed and warbled very easily, while others were shy and needed a little coaxing.

When all the pigeons had completed their solos, David said, "That was great. Now I want you to do one more thing."

Penelope asked sternly, "What about a gift for Baby Jesus?"

David chuckled and replied, "Be patient, Penelope. We're getting there."

Raising his arms, David said, "When I drop my arms, I want you all to coo and warble together."

With that, David dropped his arms, and the stable was filled with the most beautiful sound of coos and warbles.

All the animals in the stable stopped what they were doing, lifted their heads, and listened to the beautiful pigeon chorus.

"That was beautiful," praised David.

"Yeah, we did sound pretty good," admitted Penelope.

"Is that our gift?" asked one of the pigeons.

"Yes, it is," replied David. "You all practice for a few minutes before you go to sleep each night."

"When Baby Jesus comes, we can coo and warble for him," added one of the pigeons.

"Your beautiful sounds will be a lullaby for Baby Jesus. You'll help his mother get the babe to sleep."

That night after the pigeons settled onto their roosts, the stable was filled with their melodic sounds. The pigeons were practicing, and as each bird drifted off to sleep, they dreamt of entertaining Mary, Joseph, and Baby Jesus with their perfect gift.

December 19-The Web Gift Is Complete

It's almost time for Baby Jesus to arrive, so we better check on Burt and Barb and see how their project is progressing. Remember them? They are the two spiders that are working on a secret web-spinning project.

We locate the two spiders resting on the most gigantic spider web that either one of them has ever spun.

"It's looking pretty good," stated Burt.

"Yes, and we're getting it done just in time. Mary and Joseph should arrive in a couple of days."

"Hopefully the pigeons won't fly through the web again," said Burt. "They really made a mess of things last time they did that."

"That's for sure," said Barb. "All the animals in the stable scolded the pigeons, so hopefully it won't happen again."

"I hope the message we spun in the web shows up clearly."

"Andrew told us there will be a bright star over the stable when Baby Jesus is born," said Barb. "That should provide plenty of light for the web message to be seen."

Night had fallen, and the moon was full. As the moonlight passed through the giant web, a shadow of the web fell on the manger where Baby Jesus would soon lie.

Before the web masterpiece is revealed, let's take a few minutes to share what you think the image on the web will be. If you were a spider, what image would you spin on this special web?

Here's a hint. The spiders had spun four large letters in the center of the web. What do you think these four letters will spell?

As the moonlight passed through the web, the four letters—L, O, V, E—shown on the manger's surface. No other word could better describe why Baby Jesus was coming to earth. No matter who we are or what we've done, Jesus loves us, and He wants us to love Him in return.

Burt and Barb smiled as they viewed the message.

Well done, little spiders. Well done.

December 20–Solving the Dot-to-Dot

Complete the dot-to-dot, and it will reveal a gift from one of the stable animals. Which animals were responsible for making the gift?

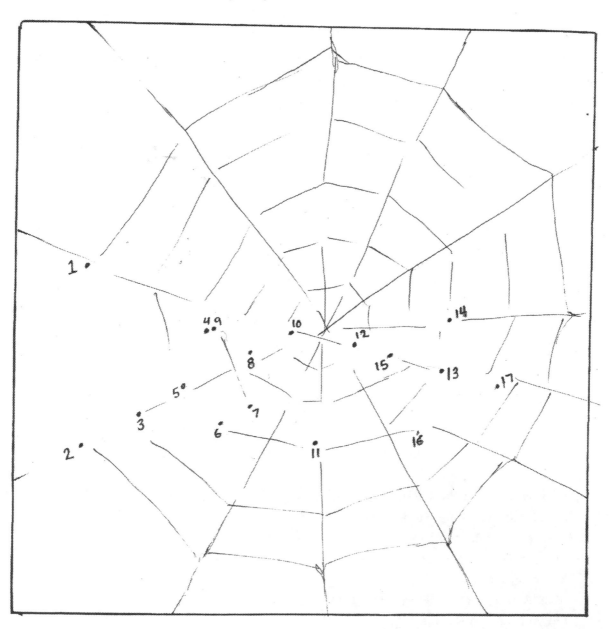

December 21–Anna Talks Beesness

Anna had completed the morning milking and decided to pull some weeds in a flowerbed bordering the stable.

She loved caring for the beautiful flowers. Often, she would bring a bouquet home for her mother or a sick neighbor.

On her knees, Anna was wrestling with a stubborn thistle plant when she heard someone call her name.

It was a tiny voice. "Anna, Anna, I need to talk to you."

At first, Anna didn't know where the voice was coming from.

"I'm here sitting on this flower petal," continued the voice.

"Oh, I see you now. You are a little honey bee."

"Yes, I am. I'm Buzz a worker bee, and I'm out gathering pollen and nectar for our hive. But our queen bee wants me to ask you a question."

"A question from the queen bee! Well, I'm honored. What is her question, Buzz?"

"The queen is excited about the arrival of the Christ Child, and she wants all of us bees to give the new family a gift."

"That's a wonderful idea. Many members in the stable are doing that too. Do you know what your gift will be?"

"Yes, we do. In fact, there are many hives scattered in the countryside surrounding the stable. All the queen bees have agreed to donate some of their honey supply to the special family. But first, all the queens need your approval."

"That's a great idea, but where will you store the honey?"

"I think I have the answer to that question. Follow me, and I'll show you a perfect storage container."

With that, the little bee flew off the flower petal and headed out into the pasture next to the stable.

"Slow down, Buzz. You're leaving me in the dust. I didn't know bees could fly so fast."

Anna had to break into a jog to keep up.

After several minutes, Buzz landed on an object partially buried in the ground, explaining, "Here's the perfect container for the honey."

"What is that?"

"It's a horn from a ram sheep that died years ago. Now the horn is almost covered with dirt."

"Do you want me to dig it up?"

"Oh, yes, if you would."

Anna found a small rock with a sharp point. She started scraping the dirt away from the horn.

Suddenly, a tiny voice shrieked, "Stop! What are you doing to our home?"

Both Buzz and Anna jumped in surprise. What animal could possibly be using a half-buried ram horn for a home?"

Tomorrow, we are going to find out whose home Anna is digging up.

But wait! Before you head off to bed, what animal's home do you think Anna is digging up? You only get one guess.

Sleep tight.

December 22–The Sweetest Gift of All

Yesterday, you read about Anna digging up a partially buried sheep horn. As the sharpened stone dug into the earth, a voice rang out, "Stop! What are you doing to our home?"

What animal did you guess was sounding the alarm? Let's continue the story and find out.

Anna peered closely at the dirt-covered horn and gasped. "Where did all of you ants come from?"

Hundreds of ants were scurrying to and fro over the exposed horn.

One of the ants replied, "We have tunnels in the soil under and inside the old horn. You will destroy our home if you keep digging with that rock."

Anna and Buzz explained their need for a container to store honey for Baby Jesus and His family.

The hundreds of ants slowed their scurrying and began to visit with each other about the problem. Finally, one of the ants said, "This is a problem we must discuss with our boss, the queen ant."

All the ants disappeared into the tunnels and were out of sight for a long time.

Finally, an ant appeared from the tunnel. The ant was larger than the worker ants and contained wings. It was the queen ant.

"Hello, Queen Ant," said Anna. "Have the worker ants explained our dilemma?"

"Yes, they have. We also heard about the Christ Child's coming, and after much discussion, we have decided to give a gift too."

"What about the ram horn?" asked Anna.

"We would like to help you dig the horn up. The horn will be our gift to the Christ Child. We will dig new tunnels and never miss the old horn."

"Oh, that would be a wonderful gift!" said Anna. "The bees thank you, and I thank you too."

Not only did the ants dig up the horn, but they removed every last speck of dirt from the inside of the horn too.

Anna carried the horn back to the stable, and she and David washed the horn until it sparkled inside and out. Then David mounted the horn on a post next to Cow's manger.

Anna announced, "The horn honey pot is now open for business."

The sky was filled with worker bees flying from their hives to the stable, bearing honey to be added to the horn honey pot. Soon the honey pot was filled to the brim.

But the worker bees knew their job was not yet complete. Once the holy family arrived, the bees would continue to keep the horn honey pot full, ensuring that the family would always have a tasty snack available.

How sweet it was.

December 23—Word-Find Fun

Directions:

Locate the words in the word find. The animals and humans that gave a gift will be in the horizontal lines of letters (letters going across). Circle the words when you discover them.

The gifts that were given will be in the vertical lines of letters (letters going up and down). Circle the gifts when you discover them.

Happy hunting!

```
T Q W F H S Y B E E S X L B J L M L A N T S
R J S X M Q F K J R U T X Z V A W D G Y B I
E L Q B K O U F H O M R T H N F J S H E C L
E M I L K M A I D — A N N A L R L W O K I E
— J V A E G I S N D O N K E Y — D A N Q T N
D H G N P J P D H S V I R T P I U R E R W C
E M W K F J L U Y B G M E O X A Q B Y A Z E
C Z A E G V Z C F L J A W I M P S L O M H K
O D W T Y K N E N R Q N T V X G Y E U — W P
R O O S T E R M C G J G B E H R I S L H Z I
A X O N E — H U M P D E M Q U A R — S O N L
T C L B C A D F K P T R V X Z N B A W R Y L
I K X O F C O W I L D H O Q K D E N C N L O
O A B A G E C J M P I G E O N S N D A P O W
N Y S W R D U X C V F Q O M H O E — M P V I
S T Z S T A B L E — M I C E K N R C E S E L
Y B D G J R O G E R — R A T N T V O L X — U
F U Z Z Y — A N D — W O O L Y W Y O — Z W A
A F J M B T H Q S V D X U Z E I P S T N E O
S P I D E R S — B U R T — A N D — B A R B C
C G K T Y E R W E I K O M R Y W T P L D H A
F L J N Q E U D A V I D S V Z C F X K B L G
```

December 24—Gift-Sharing Time

Dan the donkey came trotting into the stable and announced, "The inn is full. I just carried the baggage for the last visitor they have room for."

"There is still room in my manger," replied Cow. "In fact, David filled it with soft hay this morning."

"Mary and Joseph should arrive this evening," chimed in Roger Rat. "I can't wait! I can't wait!"

"Our spider web is ready," announced Burt and Barb.

The chickens were so proud of Tuffy because that morning he did not crow for the first time. He said he was practicing for the approaching weeks of silence.

David straightened the crown on top of the cedar tree, and the mice shook the dust off the garlands and the bows that decorated the tree.

One Hump the camel practiced talking camel to the sheep. All the sheep agreed his camel talking was "b-a-a-a-d." But they urged him to keep practicing because the three wise men and their camels wouldn't be arriving for several days. They were sure One Hump would be a wonderful host after a few more days of practice. One Hump agreed.

Anna folded the angel blanket and placed it in the manger with Roger Rat's feather pillow.

The honeybees buzzed around the ram horn, making sure no one sampled the honey before the holy family arrived.

Throughout the day, the pigeon choir could be heard practicing their coos and warbles. Their melodic sounds were a reminder of the upcoming birth of Baby Jesus.

The stable was filled with excitement.

Suddenly the familiar bright light appeared, and once again Andrew the angel was standing among the stable animals.

"You have all done a wonderful job recognizing and using your gifts to welcome Baby Jesus. Thank you! God wants each one of you to know that He loves you very much. Because of your unselfish efforts, you have made the stable worthy of being the birthplace of God's Son. God bless all of you."

Again, darkness returned to the stable as Andrew disappeared for the last time.

Sleep did not come easily for the stable animals that night. They knew that when they awoke the next morning, the most important gift of all would have arrived, Baby Jesus, the Savior of the world.

So, the first Advent is complete. Now it is time for you to follow the examples of the stable animals and go to bed too.

As you are lying in bed waiting for sleepy time to arrive, think back on all the gifts the stable animals gave to Baby Jesus.

We all have gifts that we are given. Just like David, Anna, and the stable animals, God wants us to use our gifts to honor Him.

What are your talents or gifts? They can lead you to become an artist, musician, athlete, minister, teacher, businessperson, or mechanic. There are many, many more jobs, too numerous to mention.

Begin to recognize your gifts. Ask your family members or caregivers for help. Then pray to God for inspiration about choosing a job that will allow you to use your gifts to honor Him.

Merry Christmas!

About the Artist

Janine Schmidt grew up in Wheaton, Minnesota, and earned her bachelor of fine arts degree from the Minneapolis College of Art and Design in 1989. She moved back to Wheaton, where she married Alan Schmidt. They have three children, Hannah, Nora, and Nelson. Janine does a variety of different kinds of artwork, but her favorite is illustrating children's books, especially for Mike Larson, her former biology teacher at Wheaton High School.

About the Author

Michael J. Larson spent forty-two years educating students about God's beautiful world as a biology teacher. He and his wife, Kathie, have three children and eight grandchildren. They live on a small acreage in western Minnesota, where the author blogs, gardens, plays golf, reads, and enjoys the peace and quiet of the outdoors. He can be contacted by email at mklarson@frontiernet.net or his website: www.authormichaeljlarson.com.

Printed in the United States
By Bookmasters

Printed in the United States
By Bookmasters